Josh and Dottie McDowell

NEW FRIENDS, GOOD FRIENDS?

Illustrated by Kathy Kulin Sandel

Chariot Books™
David C. Cook Publishing Co.

To Sean: A mom and dad

could not be more proud of a son.

We thank God for you.

Chariot Books™ is an imprint of David C. Cook Publishing Co.
David C. Cook Publishing Co., Elgin, Illinois 60120
David C. Cook Publishing Co., Weston, Ontario
Nova Distribution Ltd., Newton Abbot, England

NEW FRIENDS, GOOD FRIENDS?
© 1992 by Josh and Dottie McDowell for text and Kathy Kulin Sandel for illustrations

Art direction by Nancy L. Haskins
Edited by Julie Smith

First Printing, 1992
Printed in the United States of America
96 95 94 93 92 5 4 3 2 1

Library of Congress Cataloging-in-Publication Data

McDowell, Josh
New Friends, Good Friends? / Josh and Dottie McDowell: [illustrated by Kathy Kulin Sandel.]
        p.   cm.
   Summary: After making fun of a teacher in order to get his classmates to like him, Sean does the right thing with the help of his parents and their prayers. Includes discussion questions.
   ISBN 1-55513-423-8
   [1. Peer pressure–Fiction. 2. Christian life–Fiction. 3. Parent and child–Fiction.] I. McDowell, Dottie II. Kulin, Kathy Sandel, ill. III. Title.
PZ7.M478446To 1992
[E]—dc20

91-46662
CIP AC

DEAR PARENTS,

God has given us such an important responsibility—caring for and raising our children. And teaching our children now to resist peer pressure will help determine their adult behavior in years to come.

Every child faces peer pressure. Peer pressure is essentially that inward desire to be accepted by your peers. In our story, Sean's pressure to be accepted leads him to unacceptable behavior.

Research has shown that the pressure to conform, to be like the crowd, or to be accepted by another is one of the contributing factors to teenage involvement in drugs, alcohol, and premarital sexual activity. Even when children are young, they are affected by so many influences to "be like the crowd." But while they are young, they are moldable. What an opportunity for us to help them conform to Christlike behavior. "And do not be conformed to this world, but be transformed by the renewing of your mind . . . " (Romans 12:2 NKJV)

Josh & Dottie McDowell

Sean balanced a fork on the end of his finger as he listened to Dad. He loved it when Dad took him and his brother Matt out for breakfast.

"Do you care what other kids think of you?" Dad was asking them.

Matt and Sean nodded and said, "We sure do."

"Why is that?" Dad asked.

Matt spoke first. "If other kids don't like me, it makes me feel bad."

"I know how that feels, too," Sean said sadly. "Sometimes Blake and Mike, on my soccer team, don't like me. They won't be my friends."

"It hurts sometimes to be left out, and it's okay to want others to like you," Dad answered. "But remember who always loves you, no matter what."

Sean smiled. "Jesus, right?"

Dad smiled back at Sean. "Right. Jesus and your mom and me."

"Sometimes even your brother thinks you're okay," Matt said as he pushed Sean jokingly. Sean grinned and pushed back.

Matt and Sean were still teasing each other when Dad said, "Let's go, boys. We can't have you late for school." These mornings with Dad always went too fast.

Spelling. Reading. Music. Won't the morning ever
end? Arithmetic next. Boring. Boring. BORING.

Sean looked at the page of subtraction problems.
Too bad breakfast with Dad couldn't have lasted all
day. Maybe next time Dad took them out, they could
talk Dad into letting them skip school and go to a ball
game. Or maybe—

Suddenly Sean sat up and listened. Why was Mrs. Carlson so upset with Mike and Blake? Had they forgotten their homework again?

Mrs. Carlson was really scolding them.

Hey, that's not fair, Sean thought.

I wish I could do something for them.

Mrs. Carlson turned to write Mike's and Blake's names on the board. Quickly Sean stuck his tongue out at Mrs. Carlson's back.

A wave of heads turned toward Sean, and he saw his teammates give him a weak smile. A few kids giggled quietly, poking each other and pointing at Sean.

But when Mrs. Carlson turned back to the class, everyone, including Sean, was ready to begin arithmetic.

At recess, everyone gathered around Sean. "Do it again, Sean," Blake said.

"Yeah, when she lines us up for gym class!" Mike added as he slapped Sean on the back.

Sean felt pretty good. He liked having all the kids around him, and he especially liked having Mike and Blake think he was okay.

As supper ended that evening, Mom said, "Matt, you may be excused. But Sean, your dad and I want to talk to you."

"Son," Dad began in his most serious voice, "I hear that while Mrs. Carlson's back was turned, you stuck out your tongue at her. Is that true?"

Sean's eyes got as big as saucers. "How did you know?"

Mom, who taught at Sean's school, said, "I had playground duty at recess today, remember? I heard a couple of the girls in your class talking about it. Did you do it?"

"Yes."

"Why did you stick out your tongue at Mrs. Carlson, Sean?" Dad asked.

"I guess I wanted to make Mike and Blake my friends," Sean said.

"How would doing that make them your friends?" Mom asked.

Sean spoke slowly.

"Mrs. Carlson was scolding them, and I thought if I showed them I was on their side they would like me."

"Son, it is never right to do something wro[ng] to get friends," Dad said.

"Yeah, I guess you're right," Sean said sadl[y.]

"Do you think you need to apologize—to te[ll] Mrs. Carlson you're sorry?" Mom asked.

Sean nodded.

"I think the class needs to hear your apology, too," Dad added.

Sean just sat there. Supper started turning cartwheels in his stomach. *Apologize to the whole class? What will Mike and Blake think of me then?* Sean wondered.

Mom said gently, "It might help you if I write Mrs. Carlson a note so she knows what you want to do."

"I don't think this is going to be very easy," Sean said.

"I know, Sean, but Jesus will help you," Dad replied.

"Would you like to ask for His help now and tell Him you're sorry, too?" Mom asked.

"Okay," Sean said, and the three of them prayed together.

Usually Sean was anxious to get to school early to practice soccer. But not today.

Mom gave him an extra hug before he got out of the car. "I'll be praying for you, Sean. I know it will be hard," she said, handing him the note.

When Sean walked into his classroom, he went straight to Mrs. Carlson and quickly gave her the note.

Mrs. Carlson looked surprised as she read it. "Sean? Are you ready to do this now?"

Sean nodded.

As soon as the class was settled,

Mrs. Carlson called Sean to the front of

the room. He looked at everyone, then at the floor.

Could everyone see his knees shaking? Probably Mike and Blake—

in the back of the room—could hear his heart pounding.

Finally, he took a deep breath and began. "Ah, . . . I'm . . . uh . . ."

He stopped and tried to swallow. Starting over, he said as fast as he

could, "Yesterday I did something to Mrs. Carlson that was unkind.

It was wrong and I'm sorry. I won't do it again—ever."

He ran to his seat and stared straight ahead. What were the other kids thinking now? What were Mike and Blake thinking?

Mrs. Carlson said, "Sean, that was a very brave thing to do. I accept your apology."

As Sean turned slightly,

he heard Mike whisper to Blake,

"Boy, did that take guts!"

Mrs. Carlson went on, "Class, how do we show Sean that we

accept his apology?"

Mike and Blake looked right at Sean and smiled as they and

the rest of the class began clapping their hands.

At recess, Sean saw Mom across the playground. She waved, and he went over to her. "Sean, Mrs. Carlson just told me what you did. You're one great kid! It took a lot of courage to stand up there and apologize. I'm proud of you, and Dad will be, too."

Sean gave her a big smile. He had done what was right even if it meant losing his new friends. But Mike and Blake wanted to be his friends after all. They had asked him to play soccer with them at recess.

Mom smiled back at Sean and said, "Go have a good rest of the day in class. I love you."

As Sean ran back across the playground, he called to Mike and Blake, "Race you to the fence!"

Maybe today would turn out pretty well after all.

- What did Dad talk to the boys about at breakfast?

- Why did Sean stick his tongue out at the teacher?

- How did Sean's parents help him? How do your parents help you when you do something wrong?

- How could Sean have tried to make friends with Mike and Blake without doing something wrong? How can you try to make friends with someone who doesn't like you?

Parenting Suggestions from Josh and Dottie McDowell

As parents we can take time to help our children deal with peer pressure. Here are some ideas we have found helpful. The first step we have taken is to realize that peer pressure is far more a *pressure from within* to be accepted by "the group" *rather than a temptation to do something wrong.* Therefore we take specific steps to let our children know we accept them for who they are rather than for what they do. If they truly feel accepted by us, their chances of doing something wrong to be accepted by their peers is reduced.

One way to communicate acceptance is to praise effort more than success. Focus on your children's qualities such as determination, persistence, or diligence rather than their deeds. Do this especially when they fail to perform successfully. The more *you* convince them of their acceptability, the less they will require it from their peers.